MARTA.
BIG & SMALL

Jen Arena

ILLUSTRATED BY
Angela Dominguez

SCHOLASTIC INC.

Marta is una niña . . .

. . . an ordinary girl.

To a bug, Marta is grande.
Big, very big.

To an elephant,
Marta is PEQUEÑA.
Small, very small.

To a horse,
Marta is Lenta.

Slow, very slow.

To a turtle, Marta is rápida.

Fast, very fast.

To a lion,
Marta is tranquila.
Quiet, very quiet.

To a rabbit, Marta is ruidosa.

Loud,
very loud.

To a snake,
Marta is SABROSA.

Tasty,

very tasty . . .

Marta?

Phew!

Marta is **ingeniosa**.
Clever, very clever.

Marta is loud like  el león,

quiet like  el conejo,

fast like el caballo,

slow like La tortuga,

big like EL eLefante,

small like EL INSecto.

And clever, very clever,

like **una niña**.

MARTA is . . .

una niña — a girl

grande — big

pequeña — small

lenta — slow

rápida — fast

tranquila — quiet

ruidosa — loud

sabrosa — tasty

ingeniosa — clever

MARTA meets . . .

el insecto — the bug

el elefante — the elephant

el caballo — the horse

la tortuga — the turtle

el león — the lion

el conejo — the rabbit

la serpiente — the snake

For Dario, without you there would be no Marta.
Gracias, mi querido esposo. —J.A.

To Connie, Jen, Linda, and my family of course. —A.D.

Originally published as *Marta! Big & Small* by Roaring Brook Press

Text copyright © 2016 by Jennifer Arena
Illustrations copyright © 2016 by Angela Dominguez

ISBN 978-1-338-19021-2

10 9 8 7 6 5 4 3   18 19 20 21

Printed in the U.S.A.   40
First Scholastic edition 2017

Book design by Kristie Radwilowicz
Color separations by Embassy Graphics